Spell Sisters

ea

WITH SPECIAL THANKS TO LINDA CHAPMAN

First published in Great Britain in 2012 by Simon and Schuster UK Ltd
A CBS COMPANY

Text Copyright © Hothouse Fiction Limited 2012
Illustrations copyright © Mary Hall 2012
Designed by Amy Cooper

1 3 5 7 9 10 8 6 4 2

Simon & Schuster UK Ltd
1st Floor, 222 Gray's Inn Road
London
WC1X 8HB

Simon & Schuster Australia, Sydney

Simon & Schuster India, New Delhi

A CIP catalogue record for this book is available from the British Library.

PB ISBN: 978-0-85707-251-1
eBook ISBN: 978-0-85707-694-6

This book is a work of fiction. Names, characters, places and incidents are either the product
of the author's imagination or are used fictitiously. Any resemblance to actual people living or
dead, events or locales is entirely coincidental.

Printed and bound by CPI Group (UK) Ltd, Croydon, CR0 4YY
www.simonandschuster.co.uk
www.simonandschuster.com.au
www.spellsisters.co.uk

AMBER CASTLE

Spell Sisters

GRACE
THE SEA SISTER

Illustrations by Mary Hall

SIMON & SCHUSTER

Silver Hill

Croxton Manor

Morgana's Lair

Avalon

St. Stephen's Church

Fairview Vineyard

Woolston Manor

Sunnyvale

Clement Castle

Halston Castle

Glendale Stables

Belleview
Bridge

Spell
Sisters

On a Cliff-top . . .

Morgana Le Fay looked out across the rough sea. Her long coal-black hair tossed around her in the wind as she threw her hands up and grinned slyly. A huge wave crashed into white chalk cliffs below each time she flicked her wrist. She turned her gaze upwards. 'Come, my beauty!' she cried into the air.

A raven swooped down from the skies and

landed on one of Morgana's outstretched arms. She stroked his feathers. 'We must guard this place,' she told him. 'Those interfering human girls may have managed to free Sophia, Lily, Isabella and Amelia, but they will not be allowed to rescue any more of my sisters! I shall claim the island of Avalon as my own.' The raven cawed in agreement. Morgana's eyes glittered. 'You must help me, my dark one. If those girls come here and attempt to free Grace, you must stop them for me. Will you do that?'

The raven screamed loudly.

A cruel smile played at the corners of Morgana's mouth. 'I shall help you with my magic.'

She pointed at the raven and a bolt of black fire shot from her fingertips. It hit the bird, exploding into a cloud of sparks and making him screech in surprise. He flew into the sky and suddenly his wings began to grow. His beak became longer, his claws changed into knife-sharp talons and within seconds the raven was as big as Morgana herself.

'Now you are ready to deal with those two girls if they find their way here!' cried Morgana. 'Show them no mercy, my beauty!'

The raven screeched and Morgana laughed wildly, their voices merging together in the wind . . .

Painting Practice

Gwen pushed her dark red hair behind her ears and frowned as she looked from the pear on the wooden table to the picture she was painting. No matter how hard she tried, her picture just looked like a green and yellow blob. She groaned. 'Oh, Flora, this is silly. Why does Aunt Matilda feel we need to learn how to paint?'

'Because all young ladies should be able to

show off their artistic skills,' her cousin Flora answered with a smile. 'Just like we should be able to embroider beautifully, play a musical instrument and, of course, run a household wonderfully well! You know that's what Mother always says.'

Gwen rolled her eyes. 'Oh, Flora, you know I'd rather be able to ride brilliantly and shoot a bow and arrow accurately. This is really very dull indeed. When I am Lady of a manor I shall never ever paint a picture!' she declared, putting her paintbrush down. 'I shall just go out riding and have adventures!'

'Well, I won't be coming with you then. You'll need another companion,' Flora laughed, then grinned at her cousin slyly. 'Maybe Arthur?'

Gwen's cheeks went pink. 'Arthur and I are just friends!' she said hotly. Arthur was one of the pages at her uncle's castle. Like Gwen he had come to live at the Halston Castle a few years ago. It was normal for young boys to stay away from home at another noble household to learn how to be a knight, just as it was usual for young girls to do the same and learn how to be a young lady.

Flora's blue eyes twinkled. 'Just friends? I saw you going into the woods yesterday to shoot your bows and arrows together. I think he likes you, Gwen!' Flora began to twirl in front of her picture, clutching her hands together and swooning romantically. 'I think it's wonderful – you shouldn't be embarrassed. Besides. . . oh bother!' she exclaimed, as she knocked over her pot of water. 'Goodness, I really must try to be less clumsy!'

Gwen hurried over, relieved the mess had

distracted Flora from teasing her about Arthur. 'Here, I'll help,' she said, picking up an old rag and mopping the water. 'I like *your* painting though, Flora,' Gwen said catching sight of her cousin's picture. 'Those ones are good too,' she said pointing to four others nearby that Flora had also painted. She sighed. 'I don't paint as well as you do. I'm not cut out for it!'

'You just need to practise more,' said Flora.

'But practising is so boring,' said Gwen. 'I just want to go outside!' She went to the window and looked out longingly. They were up on the second floor of the castle and had fine views of the surrounding countryside. The sky was bright blue with white clouds travelling gently across. Gwen's eyes scanned over the grassy keep, drawbridge and gatehouse. Beyond the castle walls were the archery butts, stable yard, orchard and the cottages where the villagers lived. Gwen's gaze reached the thick forest to the south. She pictured the Lake that was hidden there among the trees.

'I've been thinking, Flora – Nineve's not been in contact with us for days,' she said, her hand reaching for the silver necklace around her neck. A large pendant hung from it, with a stone as blue as the ocean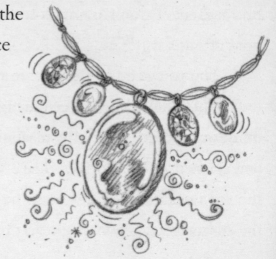

on a sunny summer's day. Four smaller gems nestled next to the pendant – a white fire agate stone with a heart of bronze, a glowing green emerald, a golden piece of amber and a glittering purple amethyst. 'I think we should go and see if there is any news on the four sisters who are still trapped. I want another adventure!'

'Sssh!' said Flora hastily. 'Mother might come in at any moment.'

Gwen quietened down, but her thoughts tumbled over each other like water in a fast-flowing stream. A little while ago she and Flora had gone to the Lake in the forest together and found the necklace with the blue pendant trapped in a rock. Flora hadn't been able to free it, but when Gwen had touched it, it had come out of the rock easily.

Gwen thought back to that moment she had

freed the necklace, remembering the beautiful woman who had risen up through the waters – Nineve, the Lady of the Lake. She had told the girls that the enchanted island of Avalon, in the centre of the Lake, was in desperate trouble. The evil sorceress, Morgana Le Fay, had trapped her eight younger sisters who lived on Avalon throughout the kingdom. If the sisters were not rescued and returned to the island by the next lunar eclipse, Morgana would claim Avalon for herself and disaster would fall on the kingdom. The stars had foretold that a mortal girl who could pull the pendant from the rock would be able to help save the sisters. Gwen was that girl. She and Flora had promised Nineve to do all they could to help, and so far they had rescued four sisters but four were still trapped.

We'll free them all! Gwen thought

determinedly. She looked out at the forest. If only Nineve would call them to her soon. . .

She picked up her brush again, an idea suddenly flashing through her mind. 'Painting would be better if I could paint something more exciting than a pear!' She quickly took another piece of parchment.

'What are you going to paint?' Flora asked curiously.

'Watch.' Gwen quickly started painting the Lake, surrounded by trees. She added a purple mist floating over the centre of the Lake hiding Avalon, and then started drawing Nineve standing on the water. She was definitely a lot more fun to paint!

'Gwen! Stop!' said Flora in alarm. 'What if Mother comes in and sees – she'll ask all sorts of questions!'

Gwen hesitated, her brush pausing over her painting. Flora was right. They weren't supposed to tell anyone about the Lady of the Lake or the Spell Sisters of Avalon.

Just at that moment, there was the sound of footsteps on the stairs. Gwen reached to crumple up her painting, but it was too late. The door opened and Flora's mother, Gwen's Aunt Matilda, came in, her golden dress billowing out behind her.

'Well, my dears, how are you getting on with your painting?' she said. Aunt Matilda was beautiful and always very elegant and well-groomed. That day her blonde hair was coiled into a bun and secured with a golden hairnet to match her dress.

'Look at mine, Mother!' Flora said, quickly, trying to distract her from Gwen.

'Very good, child,' her mother said, going over and looking at Flora's picture. 'And how about you, Guinevere?' she said, turning.

'I . . . um. . .' Gwen stammered, the painting of Nineve in her hands.

'Is that your painting?' Aunt Matilda walked over. 'Well, let me see.' Gwen had no choice but to hold it out. Aunt Matilda blinked as she looked at it. 'Hound's teeth!' She peered more closely. 'It appears to be a picture of a lady walking on water! My goodness, child. Wherever did you get such an idea?'

Gwen gulped. 'Well . . . um. . .'

Aunt Matilda raised her perfectly arched eyebrows. 'Clearly you have been listening to far too many of the minstrels' old tales and songs. I asked you to draw a pear, not make up such a ridiculous scene.'

'But Mother, Gwen did draw a pear!' said
Flora hastily. She picked up the pile of her other
drawings sneakily and waved them at her mother.
'When she knew she could draw a pear, she

decided to try something else.'

'Oh.' Aunt Matilda looked at the other paintings. 'Well, these do look like they have a certain skill and artistry, Guinevere,' she said examining them. 'Well done. You must continue with your still-life paintings though, not such nonsense as this!' she indicated Gwen's painting of the lake again. Gwen smiled at Flora gratefully.

'Now,' Aunt Matilda continued, looking around. 'Let me see. What should you paint next. . .?'

'I know!' Gwen offered.

Her aunt gave her a questioning look.

'Maybe Flora and I could go and gather some wild flowers from the forest.' Gwen put on her most obedient voice. 'Flowers are very becoming for a young lady to paint, are they not, Aunt Matilda?'

Her aunt looked pleased. 'Indeed they are. I am glad to see you thinking in such a way, Guinevere. Very well, you may go and gather some flowers for your next paintings.'

'Oh, thank you, Aunt Matilda!' cried Gwen in delight, forgetting her lady-like voice. She ran to the door. 'Come on, Flora!'

'Don't dawdle. Be back soon,' called Aunt Matilda.

'We will!' the girls chorused as they escaped.

'We're going out!' Gwen whispered as they reached the top of the stairs, her green eyes shining.

'To pick flowers in the woods so we can paint them,' Flora reminded her.

Gwen gave her a mischievous look. 'I know. But I think there might be some really *perfect* flowers by the Lake!'

Flora grinned. 'You know, I think you might just be right!'

Laughing, they raced down the stairs.

Magic Water

The girls went to their bedchamber and pulled on their tough outdoor boots and wool travelling cloaks. Gwen slung her bow over her shoulder.

'You've grown a whole head since last year,' Flora commented. 'Your bow is getting much too small for you. You should see if there are any other bows in Father's armoury you could use.'

Gwen sighed. 'I know, it is getting a bit too small for me, but it's still my favourite.' She'd had so many adventures with her bow, it felt like a lucky charm. She didn't think she was ready for a new one. Gwen tied the quiver of arrows firmly around her waist. 'Come on! Let's go!'

They ran down the stone staircase and outside into the crisp autumn air. Gwen was glad of her warm outdoor cloak. The sun was shining but there was little warmth in its rays. Overhead, a flock of glossy starlings were chirping to each other.

Flora and Gwen ran across the short grass of the keep. Over to one side the pages were practising their wrestling, but Gwen and Flora didn't stop. They were both too eager to get to the lake.

They ran across the wooden drawbridge

and down the hill towards the woods. Red, gold and yellow leaves carpeted the ground under the trees, crunching under the girls' boots.

'I wonder if Nineve has found another sister yet!' Gwen said eagerly to Flora.

'Probably not, or she would have contacted us,' said Flora. So far Nineve had always used the pendant to speak to the girls whenever she had found where another sister was trapped. 'But it will be lovely to see her and find out if she does know anything more, or – Ouch!' she gasped, tripping over a hidden tree root.

Gwen grabbed her hand and pulled her up. Flora dusted the leaves down from her skirt and they ran on.

The path twisted and turned, leading deeper into the trees until they finally burst into a large clearing. In the centre was the Lake, its surface shining like a looking glass. A purple mist hung over the middle of the water, hiding Avalon itself. The air in the clearing felt still and peaceful – *magical!*

'Nineve!' Gwen called eagerly, running to the water's edge.

A flash of silver shivered across the waters, and slowly they parted. A beautiful young woman rose up from the depths. Her long chestnut hair fell all the way to her bare feet and her robes shimmered blue and green. A pearl headband held her hair back from her face. 'Guinevere! Flora!' she said in delight. With a warm smile she ran towards them across the surface of the water as if she was running over solid ground. She stopped beside the rocks but took care not to leave the Lake. Gwen and Flora knew she had to stay in the water, or the spell she had cast to prevent Morgana crossing to Avalon would weaken and break.

'It's lovely to see you both,' Nineve said.

Gwen quickly kicked off her boots and

waded into the water to meet her. Flora followed more cautiously, carefully undoing her boots and holding her dress up high, gasping as the cold water froze her toes.

Nineve greeted them both affectionately, embracing them warmly. 'What a nice surprise! Were you out walking in the woodland?'

'Well, sort of! We were wondering if you had any news,' said Gwen. 'Have you found out where any of the other four Spell Sisters are trapped?'

'Alas, I have not managed to discover anything.' Nineve's forehead wrinkled anxiously. 'And time is running out. Soon the lunar eclipse will be here and my spell of protection over the Lake is fading. Only the strength of all *eight* sisters will be enough to prevent Morgana from taking Avalon. I wish I could find out where the remaining four sisters are trapped, but none of my magic seems to be helping at the moment.'

She looked so unhappy that Gwen squeezed her hand. 'Oh, Nineve, don't worry.'

Flora nodded. 'I'm sure you'll find out something soon.'

'I just hope it will be soon enough.' Nineve's eyes filled with tears. 'Avalon has a very important role to play in the kingdom's future. Morgana must not be allowed to succeed.' Tears spilled down her cheeks and dropped into the lake.

'She won't!' declared Gwen. 'We won't let her take Avalon, Nineve. We won't!'

Flora suddenly gasped. 'Look at the water!'

They all looked down. A silvery tear shape was floating in the water between them, glowing. As they watched it started to grow. They stepped back. 'What's happening?' breathed Gwen.

'I . . . I believe it's my water magic!' exclaimed Nineve.

The tear began to dissolve, and in its place a picture formed on the Lake's surface. It showed a white cliff with sea at the foot of it.

'I know that place!' said Gwen in astonishment. 'They're the cliffs by Woolston Manor – my parents' manor house! I used to play there when I was growing up.'

'But why are we being shown it?' asked Flora, looking at Nineve.

'One of the Spell

Sisters must be trapped there!' Nineve's face was alight. 'It will be Grace, I think. She has great power over water and that would explain why my tears conjured the image.' She looked at the girls. 'Please will you go to those cliffs and see if you can find her?'

'Of course we will, but it's quite far away – a whole day's ride – but we might be faster if we rode Moonlight,' Gwen said, thinking of the magical white stallion. He lived in the forest and helped them on lots of their recent adventures. He could travel faster than any normal horse. 'We still won't be able to get there and back and rescue Grace in a day, though. . .'

'We can't be out overnight,' said Flora anxiously. 'Mother will never allow it.'

Nineve looked worried.

'I haven't been home for a long

time,' Gwen said, thinking fast. 'Perhaps I could suggest going for a visit? Then we wouldn't need to worry about getting there and back in a day.'

Flora nodded. 'And I could say I want to come with you because I want to see my aunt and uncle and meet cousin Eleanor again – she was so little when I saw her last. It's true, it would be lovely to see them.'

Gwen smiled as she thought about her younger sister, Eleanor. She was almost as much of a tomboy as Gwen! It would be wonderful to visit her family again. 'Let's get back to the castle right now and ask Aunt Matilda if we can go,' she said eagerly.

'We'll do our best to find Grace as quickly as we can, Nineve. We promise,' said Flora.

'Thank you,' Nineve said gratefully. 'But

please be careful. Morgana will be bound to have a plan to guard Grace. She will try and stop you in whatever way she can.'

Gwen and Flora nodded. Morgana had thrown many dangers at them when they had been rescuing the other sisters – ferocious wolves, enchanted winds and angry hornets to name just a few.

Nineve took the girls' hands and squeezed their fingers. 'May Avalon's magic protect you,' she told them.

The girls stepped out of the water, dried their feet on the grass and pulled on their stockings and boots.

Nineve raised her hand. 'Farewell!'

With a flash of silver light she sank down into the water again.

Flora looked at Gwen. 'Now we just need

to talk Mother into letting us visit your house. . .'

'We'll persuade her.' Gwen raised her chin. 'We have to! Let's go!'

3

Back at the Castle

Aunt Matilda was busy dealing with household affairs when Gwen and Flora got back from the lake. The two girls went to the upstairs chamber and talked about rescuing Grace, waiting impatiently for suppertime.

'We should try and look particularly neat and tidy so that Mother will be in a good mood when we ask if we can visit your parents,'

Flora said. 'Let me do your hair tonight for once, Gwen.'

Gwen sighed. 'All right.'

Flora brushed Gwen's hair until it shone. Then she lent her a jewelled clip to hold it off her face and plaited it down her back in one long braid. She finished by threading green ribbon through it to match Gwen's dress. Gwen hardly recognised herself when she looked in the looking glass. 'I don't look like me!' she said in astonishment.

'No, but Mother will be pleased,' said Flora, as she re-plaited her own long golden braids and secured them neatly with blue ribbon.

Hearing the clang of the gong that told them it was suppertime, they went downstairs. The household always ate together in the Great Hall, a massive, high-ceilinged room with a huge stone fireplace at one end and two wooden tables. Aunt Matilda and Uncle Richard always sat at the top table and Gwen and Flora would sit near them with the pages and Uncle Richard's squire, Gareth.

Now that it was autumn, it was already dark outside and the room was lit by hundreds of candles in metal holders on the walls, giving off a strong scent. Rushes covered the floor and an enormous fire was crackling in the stone fireplace. Metal goblets and plates gleamed with a dull glow in the candlelight.

The boys were all sitting together, with the oldest page, Will, telling a story about the earlier wrestling contest that he had won. Gwen's friend Arthur was sitting near the end of the table. She saw him look in surprise at her neatly plaited hair. She grinned as she passed by on her way to

sit by her Aunt Matilda. She knew she'd have to
explain to him at some point why she was looking
so neat and tidy for once!

'Well, Guinevere,' said Aunt Matilda. 'I do

like your hair this evening. It is very becoming.'

'Thank you, Aunt Matilda,' Gwen replied in her most polite voice.

Aunt Matilda gave her an approving look. 'I believe we shall turn you into a young lady yet.'

'So, does that mean you'll be swapping your bow and arrow for tapestry work, Guinevere?' said Uncle Richard warmly. 'I hope not, for you have more skill with your bow than many of my pages!' He laughed heartily and looked at the boys. Arthur grinned, but some of the other pages – particularly Will – looked annoyed. They didn't like the fact that Gwen, a girl, was better than them with a bow and arrow.

Gwen glowed with pride. 'Oh, no, Uncle Richard, I won't be giving up archery.' She glanced quickly at her aunt. 'After all, it is acceptable for noble women to use bows and arrows isn't it,

Aunt Matilda? My mother still does.'

'Yes, my sister has always been very good at archery.' Aunt Matilda smiled and shook her head. 'You are very like she was at your age, my dear.'

Flora suddenly spoke up. 'Poor Gwen. You must miss your mother a lot.'

Gwen realised Flora had spotted an opportunity, and widened her green eyes innocently. 'Oh, I do,' she said, nodding solemnly. 'I love living here with you,' she added quickly to Aunt Matilda and Uncle Richard, not wanting to offend them. 'I am learning so much. But I do miss my family, of course. It is almost a whole year since I saw my little sister, Eleanor. She will be eight now.' She sighed sadly.

Her aunt's usually stern face softened. 'That is true. We must arrange for you to visit your family. Perhaps we could all go together?' she said, glancing at her husband. 'I would like to see my sister Alice again, too. . .'

'Or maybe just Flora and I could go,' Gwen said swiftly. She knew it would take ages for her aunt to organise the entire household to leave and visit her parents' manor house. She and Flora couldn't wait that long to rescue Grace.

'Oh, yes!' Flora exclaimed. 'I would dearly love to see my aunt and uncle and little cousin Eleanor, Mother.'

Aunt Matilda looked thoughtful. 'Well, there would also be plenty of opportunities for you both to practise your painting skills on a visit to the coast. What do you think, Richard?'

'I think it's an excellent plan!' Flora's father agreed. 'Flora could benefit from the riding practise too. Two days in the saddle will be good

for her. Gareth shall go with them to keep watch
– not that Guinevere needs much protection!'
Uncle Richard threw a smile at his niece and
then turned back to his wife. 'You can arrange a
full family visit for another time, my dear. I have
business here for the next month and cannot be
away. If the girls only stay for a few days they will

be able to carry everything they need in saddle bags. I think they can go as soon as tomorrow, we can send a rider on ahead first thing in the morning to warn your sister of their arrival.'

'Oh, thank you!' gasped Gwen.

Her uncle's eyes twinkled. 'You know, I have been watching you recently, Guinevere, and you may find I have a gift for you before you go!'

Gwen would normally have been excited at the thought of a present from her uncle, but right then her mind was filled with nothing but the thought of going home, seeing her family – and most of all, of a chance to rescue Grace. 'Thank you, Uncle!' she said. 'And thank you very much, Aunt,' she added again, using her most polite voice. 'I shall do my best to be a credit to you while I am at my parents' house.'

Her aunt nodded and then the conversation moved away from the two girls.

Flora caught Gwen's eye and, kicking each other under the table, they both grinned. It had worked!

4

A Gift for Gwen

The girls got up early the next morning, both keen to be off. They packed their clothes into saddlebags along with their paints and brushes and then put on their travelling clothes, fastening them with iron brooches. Gwen secured her leather quiver of arrows around her waist and slung her bow over her shoulder. She pushed her hair back over her shoulders. After a night's sleep it was back to its usual tangled state. She much preferred it that way!

'Ready to go?' Flora said, checking her reflection one last time in the glass and smoothing down a few strands of her own blonde hair.

'Definitely!' said Gwen. 'The sooner we rescue Grace the better!'

They hurried outside.

The stable master was waiting in the keep with two ponies for them. Gwen was pleased to see she would be riding Merrylegs, her favourite pony, who was a lively grey. Flora was going to be riding Willow, a sweet chestnut mare. Gareth was also there with his handsome bay horse, Star. Along with his own saddlebags he had an extra bag containing food for the journey provided by Hal, the household's cook – cold slices of spiced mutton wrapped up in cloth, oatcakes, apples from the orchard and a gourd filled with water. A long sword hung at Gareth's waist. Gwen knew that her uncle's messenger would already have been sent ahead on one of the fastest horses. He would change horses at an inn and make it there in half the time they would take walking and trotting through the forest. Gwen could imagine her family getting excited to see them already!

Suddenly Gwen heard the castle door opening and heard her uncle's booming voice.

'So, are the visiting party ready to depart?' He came out of the castle with her aunt and some of the pages.

'Yes, Father!' cried Flora. 'We're about to leave.'

'Not before I give Guinevere her present. Hayward!' Sir Richard called. Hayward, who made the castle bows, came out of the castle and Gwen caught her breath as she saw he was carrying a new bow. He handed it to Sir Richard. 'This is for you, Guinevere.' Her Uncle said, presenting the bow to her, 'I noticed the other day that your old bow is far too small for you and

I asked Hayward to make you a new one. What do you think?'

Gwen swallowed. It was beautiful, and part of her felt very excited at the thought of having a new bow, but she also loved her old one. She saw her uncle beaming with pleasure and waiting for her response. 'Thank you very much, Uncle,' she said, taking it. 'It's wonderful!' It was made of pale, smooth elm-wood and had soft brown leather wrapped around its handle. It felt heavier than her old bow.

'You'll be able to shoot farther with this one,' her uncle said, delighted. 'Look after it!'

'I will. I promise,' she said. Feeling the weight of her new bow, Gwen wondered if she would be able to shoot as well with it as her uncle hoped. What if she wasn't strong enough to use it properly?

'Now, shall I take that old bow and put it in the armoury?' asked Sir Richard. 'Maybe one of the younger pages could use it.'

But Gwen couldn't bear the thought of someone else using her beloved bow. 'Um. . .'

Just then Gareth's horse plunged excitedly, making Merrylegs and Willow shy away. Luckily, the commotion distracted her uncle.

'Well, looks like someone's eager to be off!' he said, going over to Gareth and giving his horse a hearty pat on the neck. 'Now, I have a message I would like you to carry to my brother-in-law.' While he was busy telling Gareth the message, to wish Gwen's father good health, Gwen quietly slipped her old bow on to the saddle, tying it to her saddle bags. She was going to take it with her too.

Arthur came over. 'I like your new bow,' he said admiringly.

Gwen bit her lip. 'It's good, isn't it? I just hope ... well ...' She wondered if he'd understand. 'I wonder if I'll be able to shoot as well with it.'

Arthur looked at her in surprise. 'Of course you will! You're a brilliant shot, Gwen.'

Gwen felt pleased at his words but she still couldn't help wondering if he was right.

'You know it's not your bow that makes you such a good shot,' said Arthur, seeing her face. 'It's you.'

She smiled. 'Thanks, Arthur.'

He smiled back and then said in a rush, 'I like your hair better this morning.'

Gwen caught sight of Flora. From the grin on her face it was clear she had overheard Arthur's comment. Gwen felt colour leap into her cheeks. 'We should be going,' she said hastily. 'Bye, Arthur.'

He stepped back. 'Goodbye. Travel safely!'

Finally it was time to go. Gareth led the way out of the gates with Flora and Gwen following behind. The horses' hooves clattered on the drawbridge. Flora rode Willow close to Merrylegs. 'So Arthur likes your hair better this way?' she whispered teasingly.

Gwen glared at her.

Flora opened her mouth to tease some more, but just then Gareth dug his heels into his horse's sides. His horse plunged forward. Gwen urged Merrylegs on after him. *It's time to go and rescue Grace,* she thought in excitement as they cantered down the hill. The forest loomed up in front of them. Now the adventure was really about to start!

5

Woolston Manor

Gwen and Flora followed Gareth through
the forest. He didn't talk much, but Gwen
didn't mind – she was busy thinking about Grace.
In the vision on the Lake, she had recognised
the white chalk cliffs near to her parents' manor
house, but where was Grace trapped? Was she
actually *in* the cliffs? Or somewhere at the top of
them? Maybe she was in the rocks at the bottom?

There was no telling where Morgana might have imprisoned her.

So far, all the sisters that Gwen and Flora had rescued had been disguised to make them even harder to find. Gwen's fingers went to her necklace. She just needed to get close enough to each trapped sister, touch the pendant and say the magic spell Nineve had taught her and then the sister would be free, with her magic powers restored. Gwen really hoped she could do that with Grace, too.

First we have to find her though, Gwen reminded herself. *And that probably isn't going to be easy.*

They rode out of the forest and continued along twisting country roads. They passed through hamlets and villages, trotting past cottages with thatched roofs. Stray dogs barked and ran at them, and children dressed in rags stopped to stare. At lunchtime they halted in a grove of trees and ate the lunch that Hal had prepared. They all shared some water and let the ponies have a rest and drink from a stream.

'We should press on,' said Gareth. 'It grows dark more quickly at this time of year.'

They remounted quickly and rode until Gwen smelt the familiar tang of salt and seaweed in the air at last. Her heart leaped. They must be getting closer to the sea! They were riding across heathland now, and overhead seagulls were circling and cawing. Gwen's muscles were aching from riding all day. She knew Flora was sore too from the sighs she was making and the way she kept shifting her weight in the saddle, but breathing in the sea air she felt her spirits lift.

'There it is!' The words burst from her as

they entered the village and she saw Woolston
Manor – her family home – on a slight hill
surrounded by fields and grazing land. It was
a beautiful old manor house made out of grey
stone. Merrylegs was tired, but sensing Gwen's

excitement he sped up. Not bothering to wait for Gareth, Gwen kicked him on and cantered towards the house.

As Gwen rode up, the front door burst open and three people came hurrying out – her father, Leo, her mother, Alice and her little sister, Eleanor.

Gwen reined Merrylegs in and flung herself off his back. The next moment she was caught up in her father's bear hug. He was tall with red hair just like Gwen's.

'It's so wonderful to see you!' he exclaimed.

'Oh, Father!' gasped Gwen. 'Mother!'

Gwen's father let her go and she tightly hugged her mother, who was small and slim with wild brown hair and dancing hazel eyes.

'And me?' cried a voice. 'Is it wonderful to see me too?' Eleanor was jumping up and down on the spot in excitement beside their parents.

'Oh, yes!' cried Gwen, grabbing her sister's hands and swinging her round. 'You've grown so much, Ellie!'

Her sister had their mother's brown curly hair, but her eyes were green like Gwen's and just as full of daring and mischief.

'Eleanor isn't the only one who has grown,' said their father. 'Look at you, Gwen! And is that a new bow I see on your shoulder?'

'Yes,' Gwen answered, feeling proud that she was old enough to need a new bow. 'Uncle Richard gave it to me before we left. I've still got my old one that you had made for me, though.'

Her father smiled. Suddenly Gwen remembered Flora and Gareth. She swung round. They had halted a little way off to give

the family time to greet each other. Gwen called them over.

'Here's cousin Flora and Uncle Richard's squire, Gareth.'

'Oh, Flora, how lovely to see you again.' Gwen's mother ran forward to greet Flora while Gwen's father went to talk to Gareth and ask about the journey. 'I was so delighted when the messenger arrived with news that you were coming!'

'We're so happy we had a reason to come and visit,' said Flora, and then added hastily, 'I mean, Mother thought it would be a good chance for us to practise our painting skills.'

Gwen's mother's eyes twinkled. 'It sounds like my sister hasn't changed a bit. Is she succeeding in turning you into a young lady, Gwen?'

'Only a little bit,' replied Gwen with a grin.

'She's always telling me that I am not neat and tidy and I don't care enough about household duties.'

'She used to say that to me too when I was growing up!' her mother laughed. 'But you are happy there, aren't you, my dear?' she added anxiously.

'Oh, yes – very,' said Gwen. She took Flora's hand. 'It's really good fun living with Flora and Aunt Matilda and Uncle Richard.'

'What do you do? Have you had any adventures?' Eleanor asked eagerly.

Gwen smiled at her. 'Oh, a few. . .'

'Tell me! Tell me!' begged Eleanor.

'First let your sister and Flora come inside,' said their mother. 'You two must be ready to rest and have something to eat and drink.'

'I am tired!' admitted Flora.

Gwen was tired too, but her excitement

made her aches and pains fade away. She couldn't stop looking around as they went inside. Her family's manor had always seemed big to Gwen when she was growing up, but it seemed quite small now she had grown used to Halston Castle, which was far larger. The ground floor had the kitchens, storerooms and a great hall where everyone ate and most of the household slept at night. Upstairs were her parents' private chambers and in the attic two small bedrooms for Eleanor and Gwen.

It wasn't yet time for supper, but Robert the cook brought them small pastry tarts filled with spiced mincemeat, and some bread and cheese. The girls ate hungrily, washing the food down with glasses of cool water while Gareth drank ale with Gwen's father.

Eleanor chattered away while they ate.

'I can row the rowing boat all by myself now,' she said proudly. 'And I can ride really well. I rode bareback the other day and didn't fall off. I've been having throwing competitions with Simon and Albert from the village and I beat them every time. Though they're better at running than me. Oh, and Father says I can have my own bow and arrows soon and learn how to shoot with them. But I think I'm ready *now*, don't you, Gwen? It's not fair!'

Gwen grinned as Eleanor pestered them for stories about life at Halston Castle. The questions tumbled out of her. 'How many pages are there? Do they let you join in their swordplay? Do they have to practise jousting? Have you been to many tournaments? Do you still go shooting a lot? What do—'

'Eleanor! Eleanor!' her mother interrupted with a laugh. 'Give Gwen and Flora a rest. Why don't you go and play outside for a while?'

Eleanor frowned. 'But I don't want to. . .'

'No "buts"! Gwen and Flora are tired after their journey. Go and check the horses. Then you can gather some apples in the orchard. I heard Robert saying we're running low.'

Eleanor sighed crossly but obediently took the basket her mother handed her and went outside.

Gwen smiled. 'Ellie's just the same as ever.'

'She's been beside herself with excitement ever since the messenger arrived and said you were coming to stay,' her mother said. 'She does miss you very much, Gwen.' She glanced apologetically at Flora. 'I'm afraid she's not going to leave either of you alone while you're here.'

'That's all right. We don't mind,' said Flora cheerfully.

Gwen frowned, seeing a problem. If Eleanor was going to follow them around all the time, how would they sneak away on their own to try and rescue Grace?

'So, tell me all about your aunt and uncle and how everyone is at the castle?' her mother said, interrupting Gwen's thoughts.

Gwen told her about everything that had been happening – leaving out the adventures they'd had freeing the Spell Sisters, of course. As Flora was talking about a jousting tournament they had been to recently, Gwen glanced at the window. The sun was setting now, sending pink and golden streaks across the sky. Maybe this was their chance to get down to the cliffs while Eleanor was busy gathering apples in the orchard.

'Mother, would you mind if Flora and I went for a little walk?' she asked suddenly. 'I'd really like to show her around and get some fresh air before supper.'

'Oh, yes,' said Flora eagerly, immediately working out what Gwen was planning. 'I'd love to go for a walk, Aunt Alice.'

Gwen's mother nodded. 'Of course you may

go, girls. Supper will be in about an hour. I shall organise one of the maids to take your luggage up to Gwen's room and unpack it. It'll be a squeeze in there with two beds but I thought you would prefer sleeping there to staying in the hall.'

Gwen nodded. At least if they were in her bedroom she and Flora would be able to talk about Grace without being overheard.

They went outside. Gwen saw her small travelling bag and her two bows beside the saddlebags on the ground. She took her bag and then hesitated. Making up her mind, she picked up her old bow and slung it over her shoulder. She knew she would feel happier with it.

'The cliffs are over that way,' she said, pointing to the south, past the walled orchard with its apple, pear and plum trees. 'The beach is only ten minutes away.'

'Let's go then!' said Flora.

Gwen led the way out towards the sea but as they were passing the orchard they heard some loud shouts.

'I wonder what's going on in there?' Gwen said, stopping in surprise. Going to the gate, they looked in. Eleanor was standing at the base of a tree throwing apples at a teenage boy and shouting fiercely. 'I don't care if the cook told you to put nets in the trees. I wouldn't even care if it was my *father* who told you to do it! It's cruel!' Eleanor threw apple after apple, her eyes flashing. The boy ducked and yelled out as they hit him. The little girl's aim was very accurate!

'What's happening?' Flora gasped.

Gwen spotted a large net in the branches of the trees. It was made of fine mesh, with weights around the edges. 'Eleanor's found a bird net in the trees!' she realised.

'What's a bird net?' asked Flora.

'Robert the cook uses them for trapping birds so they don't peck at the fruit growing in the orchard,' Gwen explained. 'The bids fly into the trees and when they land they get their legs and wings tangled in the net. They can't escape. The more they struggle the more tangled up they get until they break their wings or die.'

'But that's horrible!' said Flora aghast.

'I know,' said Gwen – and her sister obviously felt the same.

'Get out of this orchard right now!' Eleanor was shrieking at the boy as the apples thumped him. 'Take that! And that!' The boy finally gave

up, turned and ran out of the orchard past Gwen and Flora. As soon as he was gone,

 Eleanor started to climb up the nearest tree trunk.

'Ellie!' shouted Gwen. 'Stop!'

But the angry little girl didn't hear. She climbed up higher.

'What's she doing now?' asked Flora in alarm.

'I think she's climbing up to get the net down, but it's really high. Come on!' Gwen ran over as her sister began untangling a net near the top of the tree.

'Ellie! Come down! You're too high up!' Gwen called anxiously.

Eleanor looked down through the tree's branches. 'I will when I've got this net out!' she called, tugging at it hard. 'If I don't get it down then the birds will get caught, and I'm not going to let that happen!' She pulled the last of the net free. 'Got it!' she cried triumphantly.

Flora's hands went nervously to her mouth as the branches swayed dangerously.

'Here! Catch!' Eleanor called, throwing the net down to Gwen.

Gwen caught the net and stuffed it into her travelling bag. 'OK, I've got it. Now you come down too. Be careful.'

'Oh, climbing trees is easy!' said Eleanor airily. She started to clamber down. 'I wish mother would let me wear a tunic and breeches like a boy – it would be even easier then. Dresses are a nuisance!'

'Be careful, Ellie!' Flora called in alarm, seeing the little girl's foot reaching for a hold but finding empty space.

'I'm fine,' Eleanor said, kicking at the skirt of her dress. 'I'm almost down. I—' But then she broke off with a squeal as she lost her grip and started to fall. . .

Finding Grace

'Ellie!' gasped Gwen, dashing forwards to catch her sister. But she was too late. Eleanor landed hard on the ground, with a thud.

'Ow!' Eleanor shrieked, sitting up and grabbing her ankle.

Gwen crouched down beside her. 'Are you all right, Ellie? Are you hurt?'

'My ankle!' Eleanor cradled her foot.

'It's really hurting.' Tears filled her green eyes.

'Oh, Ellie. You poor thing.' Flora knelt beside her. 'Let me see.' Flora gently eased the younger girl's boot off and examined the foot. 'We've got to get her back to the house, Gwen. I think it might be broken.'

For a moment Gwen felt a flash of dismay as she thought about Grace. They really needed to find her, but her sister needed them more right now. She carefully helped Eleanor up. 'Put one arm round my neck and I'll help you back home,' she said gently.

It was very slow getting back to the manor house with Eleanor limping along.

'Oh dear, Eleanor!' Gwen's mother cried as they went in through the big front door. 'Whatever have you done now?'

Gwen and Flora explained. Gwen's mother

called for Hester, the kitchen maid and nurse.

'I think it is just a bad sprain and not a break, Madam,' she told Gwen's mother after she had examined Eleanor's foot, and bandaged it up with clean rags.

'Now, Eleanor, you must rest for the next few days,' Gwen's mother said, as Hester left the hall.

'But I don't want to rest. I want to show Gwen and Flora around while they're here!' Eleanor protested.

'They'll be no showing anyone anything for you,' her mother said firmly.

'It's not fair!' huffed Eleanor. 'I was only trying to help the birds, and now I have to sit and rest. It's so boring. I want to go outside with Gwen and Flora!' Even though she had been so brave with the pain, tears now welled in her eyes.

'Oh, Ellie, don't worry. We'll sit in and talk to you,' said Gwen. Flora nodded.

Lady Alice smiled. 'Thank you, girls. It's time for supper now, in any case. Eleanor you can stay down here. Gwen and Flora, why don't you go upstairs to get ready?'

Gwen nodded. She glanced at the window and felt her heart sink. It was dark outside now – there was no way they could find Grace that night. Disappointment rushed through her.

'I wish we could have gone down to the cliffs,' she whispered to Flora as they went up the winding staircase to her attic bedroom.

'Me too, but we had to help Ellie,' Flora said. 'We couldn't have left her.'

'I know.' Gwen didn't regret helping her sister but she felt worried about Grace. 'We mustn't let anything stop us tomorrow though, let's go out early. We'll get up before anyone else – I always used to do that when I was younger. Mother and Father won't worry.'

'Good plan!' said Flora.

'Come on,' Gwen said happily. 'Let's get changed!'

They hurried up the last flight of stairs. Gwen's bedchamber was small with one bed and an extra mattress on the floor. Mary had unpacked all their belongings. Gwen put her travelling bag and old bow down.

'Why did you bring your old bow when you've got a new one?' asked Flora. 'Don't you like the one Father gave you?'

'Oh, I do like it. I like it a lot!' said Gwen. 'It's just that this one feels almost like a lucky charm. Whenever we've been fighting Morgana it's always helped.'

'It's not the bow that's helped, it's your skill in shooting with it,' said Flora.

Gwen almost replied: that's just what Arthur said to me, but she bit the words back not wanting Flora to tease her about Arthur again. 'I suppose you're right,' she said.

'You should let one of the pages back home have it,' said Flora. 'One of the little ones, like Tom, would love it.'

'Mmm,' Gwen said reluctantly. She knew there was no point keeping her old bow when someone else could use it, but she just didn't want to let it go. 'I'll decide when we get back. First we have to rescue Grace.'

'Yes,' Flora agreed. 'No matter how hard Morgana tries to stop us!'

Gwen didn't sleep very well that night. She couldn't stop thinking about Grace. Where had Morgana imprisoned her? Would it be very difficult to rescue her? And what would Morgana do to try and stop them? She had let Flora sleep in her bed and was sleeping on the mattress on

the floor. It wasn't very comfortable and she tossed and turned, waking up every few hours to look towards the small attic window and see if it was morning yet. At long last the rectangle of sky through the window changed from velvet black to dove grey and she heard the sound of the first birds calling out.

'Flora, wake up!' Gwen jumped up from her mattress and shook her cousin. 'It's daybreak!'

Flora sat up sleepily. Gwen quickly took off her nightdress and pulled on her old travelling dress. 'Come on!' she urged Flora, who was still getting out of bed.

They were soon both ready to go. Gwen picked up her old bow.

'Take your new one instead!' Flora urged. 'Father said you'll be able to shoot further with it.'

Gwen hesitated.

'Come on!' Flora was by the door.

Gwen didn't want to waste time arguing. They had to find Grace. 'All right.' She gave in and picked up her new bow instead. Putting it over her shoulder, she tried to get used to the feel of the extra weight.

The cold morning air stung the girls' cheeks as they slipped out of the back door. The sun was just rising, its pale watery rays chasing away the last of the night.

They hurried through the manor grounds, past the orchard and out on to the rough heathland that led towards the sea. Skylarks flew up from their nests hidden in the grass, singing out in alarm as the girls ran past.

'I wonder where Grace will be?' panted Flora as they ran. 'I hope we'll be able to find and free her without too much trouble. . .'

Gwen pictured the cliffs. 'I think we should go down to the beach and walk along it. We may get some clue as to where Grace is.' She pointed ahead of them. 'There's a path over there that leads down to the waterfront.'

But when they reached the path, they saw that the tide was right in. The waves were breaking near the bottom of the white cliffs, hiding most of the beach from view. There were just a few small areas close to the cliffs still visible. There was no way of walking along the shore though. 'What are we going to do now?' asked Flora in dismay.

Gwen's eyes widened. 'I know! My old boat! Do you remember Ellie telling me that she had learned how to row? It must still be here somewhere if she used it recently. Come on!' She ran on down the cliff path. Sure enough, a small wooden boat with oars was tied up to a post on a patch of shingle just above the tide line. 'There it is!' Gwen said in delight. 'We can row out to take a look at the cliffs. We won't need to walk!'

Flora looked doubtful as Gwen ran over and untied it. 'Are you sure?'

'Absolutely!' said Gwen. 'The sea's calm at the moment. I'll easily be able to row us along and we can look for signs of Grace.' She handed the rope to Flora and pushed the boat down the gentle slope into the water. 'You'll need to hold on to the rope to stop the boat floating away!' she called over her shoulder. 'I'll get in and hold the boat steady with the oars, then you can get in from the rocks over there so you don't get too wet.'

Flora held on tight while Gwen pulled her skirts up, waded through the water and climbed into the boat. Her boots and stockings were soaking, but she didn't care. She picked up the oars. 'All right, Flora, you can throw the rope into the boat then get to those rocks over there!' she called.

Flora did as Gwen said, waiting on the nearby rocks while Gwen rowed over to them. Then, very gingerly, Flora stepped into the boat. She squealed as it rocked and swayed in the water. 'I'm not sure I like this!' she gasped, sitting down with a bump.

'You'll soon get used to it,' Gwen grinned. It felt brilliant to be out in her boat again. She pulled on one oar until they were facing away from the shore. The boat was swaying up and down with the waves as they came in towards the cliffs, but Gwen knew that once they got further out it would feel calmer. Flora held on tightly to the side of the boat. Gwen pulled both oars and the little boat bobbed its way through the water, heading away from the cliff. Taking a breath of sea air, Gwen felt urgent excitement surge through her. They were finally on their way to rescuing Grace!

Once they were a little way out, Gwen began to row parallel with the white cliffs. They were made of chalk, soft and crumbly with green grass growing at the top. 'Look out for anywhere that Grace might be trapped,' Gwen told Flora, who was still holding tightly to the side of the boat.

'I'll . . . I'll try. . .' Flora said shakily.

Gwen gave her a sympathetic look. 'Why don't you have a try at rowing? It might help you feel steadier. Here. Look. It's easy!'

She showed Flora how to hold the oars and pull them towards her.

'It *is* fairly easy, isn't it?' said Flora, smiling as she grew more confident – but just then one of her oars caught in the water, pulling her out of her seat and almost jerking out of her grasp. 'Oh!' she gasped.

Gwen grabbed her. 'Careful! You have to keep pulling smoothly and never let go of the oars!'

Flora nodded and tried again while Gwen's eyes scanned the cliffs. Where could Grace be?

Suddenly her eyes caught sight of something in the cliff face. Could it be . . . a figure? 'There!' Gwen exclaimed. 'Look!'

Flora followed her gaze.

'Oh, Gwen, that has to be Grace!' There in the cliff face, near the top was the figure of a young woman. She looked as if she was carved into the rock, her long hair spreading around her, her hands reaching out as if to ward off a spell.

'I need to get up there and say the spell to release her,' Gwen said urgently.

'But how will you do that?' asked Flora.

Gwen frowned. 'I'll have to climb the rocks.

Do you think you can row the boat towards the cliffs? When we're at the bottom, I'll get out and climb up. You'll have to stay here with the boat though. Will you be able to manage?'

Flora nodded, her face pale. 'I'll have to. We have to free Grace.'

'And quickly, before Morgana realises we're here,' said Gwen, looking around anxiously. 'All right – row as close to the cliff as you can and I'll get ready to jump out!' She shifted her bow on

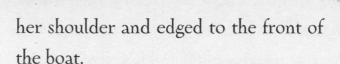

her shoulder and edged to the front of
the boat.

Flora pulled on the oars and guided the
boat towards the cliffs. Gwen took a breath.
It was going to be a dangerous climb. The cliffs
were steep, but the chalk was crumbly and soft.
Gwen was hopeful she'd be able to find foot and
hand holds as she climbed. *I have to do it. Grace
needs me to*, she thought.

But just as they were a few metres away from
the base of the cliffs, the waves got choppier, and

the boat more unsteady. 'Gwen!' gasped Flora, struggling to hold on to the oars. 'I'm not sure what's happening.'

Gwen glanced around and saw that the blue sky was turning to grey as storm clouds raced overhead. The waves rolling in behind them were growing taller by the second. 'It must be Morgana!' she exclaimed in alarm. 'I bet she's trying to stop us! Hold on, Flora! I'll take the oars.'

But as Flora tried to pass the oars over to Gwen, an enormous wave swept underneath the boat, sending it lurching to one side. Gwen grabbed on to the edge of the boat, but Flora shrieked as she was thrown out into the icy water!

'Flora!' Gwen yelled as the waves closed over Flora's head.

Under Attack!

Flora's head popped out of the raging waves. Gwen leaned over the side of the boat, reaching out for her cousin. 'Grab my hand!' she yelled over the sound of the crashing waves. 'Quickly!' Salt water splashed in her face making her eyes sting, but she ignored it. Flora spluttered, her fingers finally closing on Gwen's.

Hanging on for dear life, Gwen began to

haul Flora back into the boat. Flora kicked and grabbed on to the boat's side, before finally rolling over the edge and collapsing on to the rocking floor. She was soaked through, her hair plastered against her head, water dripping from her clothes.

'Oh, Flora!' Gwen hugged her cousin tightly, and then pulled off her own cloak, wrapping it around Flora to stop her shivering. Then Gwen hastily used the oars to steady the boat on the rolling waves. 'Come on. Maybe we should get you home?'

'No!' gasped Flora bravely. 'That's what Morgana will expect us to do, but we have to rescue Grace. I'll be all right.' She took the oars off Gwen. 'Climb up the cliff. I'll keep the boat as steady as I can, and this time I won't fall out!'

Gwen looked at her anxiously, but Flora

looked completely determined. 'All right,' she agreed. 'I'll be as quick as I can.'

With the waves still tossing the little boat around, Flora rowed to the base of the cliff once again, her face pale with the effort. Gwen waited until the boat was as far in as it could safely get and then jumped.

The icy water hit her, but the water only came up to just above her knees. She waded through and reached the base of the cliff. Glad she didn't have her heavy cloak pulling her down, she found some handholds. The chalk was crumbling, which made it easier to dig her boots in. Adjusting the bow on her back, she gritted her teeth and started to climb upwards. Grace was up there, ready to be rescued – Gwen just had to get to her before Morgana realised the storm hadn't stopped them.

Gwen moved steadily up the cliff, resisting the urge to look down. *Keep going*, she told herself, *Just keep going*. She was making good progress as, hand over hand, she climbed up the cliff face. But then suddenly over the cries of the seagulls came another sound. A harsh, loud cawing noise together with the beating of large wings.

'Gwen!' she heard Flora shout from below her.

Gwen glanced over her shoulder and felt her blood turn to ice. An enormous black raven, the size of a person, was flapping towards her. Its red eyes gleamed above its sharp beak, and it flew at Gwen as if intending to pluck her from the cliff and carry her away!

Gwen gasped in terror. Reaching a ledge in the chalk, she clambered on to it, her hands instinctively reaching for her bow and arrows.

They were the only weapons she had!

If only I had my old bow! The thought raced across her mind as she quickly notched an arrow into place. The bird was closer now – she could see its knife-like talons and its fearsome, glowing

stare. The monstrous creature could only be the work of Morgana, she knew that. Gwen pulled back the string. It felt different from her old bow: stiffer, stronger, more powerful. A moment of horrible doubt pushed into her mind. Could she shoot as accurately as she needed to with this new bow? What if she wasn't strong enough? What if she missed? Gwen remembered what Flora and Arthur had said. *They* believed in her. She had to believe in herself too. Yes, the bow was important, but not as much as her skill at using it. That was what counted above all.

Gwen steadied herself and concentrated on the raven. At last, breathing out, she relaxed and released the arrow. It cut through the air, heading for the bird with absolute accuracy.

With a furious scream, the bird dived out of

the way. It flew up and circled round. Gwen waited, her heart pounding. What was it going to do now? She notched another arrow into place in case it attacked her again. But then to her horror she saw its eyes fix on Grace, still frozen higher up the cliff face. The bird flapped its massive wings and started flying straight towards the trapped Spell Sister. It was going to try and injure Grace while she was imprisoned in the chalk!

Gwen shot another arrow, aiming this time in front of the raven's beak, trying to deflect it from its course – one arrow, two, three. She had no time for doubt any more. The arrows shot from her bow as fast as she could pull them from the quiver. The raven screeched in fury as it had to pull up in its course again.

Gwen's thoughts raced. She was going to run out of arrows. What would happen then? As she reached for the next arrow in her quiver, her hand bumped into her travelling bag. Suddenly, she remembered the net she had picked up the day before when she and Flora had helped her sister. Maybe she could use that?

Yes!

Gwen snatched it from her bag. It was made of fine mesh and had little weights sewn in around its edge so that it could be thrown or draped over a tree's branches. It certainly wouldn't cause much harm to the enormous raven, but it might at least help distract it for a little while, giving her time to climb the cliff and free Grace.

'Here! Come and get me!' she cried to the raven, waving at the bird.

The raven couldn't resist. He swooped at her.

'No, Gwen, don't!' Flora shouted from below.

Gwen held her nerve as the bird got closer and closer. She got the net ready. The raven didn't seem to notice, it was so focussed on getting to her. She could feel the wind from its wings. Its beak opened, and from down in the boat she could hear Flora let out a terrified scream.

Now! Gwen thought, and she threw the net with all her strength. The net sailed through the air like a great spider's web and landed on the raven's head, covering his neck and back too. The evil bird cawed in surprise and flapped frantically as it tried to free its wings, but the net tangled around them. The bird started to fall towards the sea, but Gwen had her bow ready. She aimed and launched an arrow into the air before pulling out another arrow, then another, firing rapidly.

They zipped towards the bird, catching the net and slamming hard and deep into the cliffs curving around the coastline. The arrows' force pulled the raven with them. The raven fought and shrieked as the net and arrows pinned it against the cliff. Desperate to break free, it began to rip through the fine mesh with its beak.

Gwen knew there wasn't a second to lose. The raven could escape at any moment! She began to climb as quickly as she could. Her fingers dug into the chalky surface of the cliff as her toes desperately kicked footholds out of the soft rock. Just above her was another ledge, jutting out a little below where Grace was frozen in the cliff face. Gwen could hear the raven shrieking below but she didn't pause to look down.

'You can do it, Gwen!' Flora cried up to her.

Gwen reached the ledge and hauled herself

up on to it, wondering for one horrible moment
if the rocky shelf might break off. But thankfully
it was thick and strong, and held fast. Panting and
gasping, she stood up. Grace was there in front
of her – her outline clear in the white surface of
the cliff.

Gwen pulled her pendant out and pushed the blue stone against Grace's body. She quickly began the chant Nineve had taught her:

'Spell Sister of Avalon, I now release.
Return to Avalon and help bring peace!'

A silver flash ran across the figure in the cliff, and Gwen caught her breath as the chalk in front of her started to crumble away.

8
Rescue!

The chalk showered down like snow, magical and shimmering, and then finally Grace stepped out of the cliff-face and on to the ledge beside Gwen. The fifth Spell Sister of Avalon was just as beautiful as the others, with long dark hair and a heart-shaped face. Her sea-green eyes were startled and confused, and a fine white dust covered her turquoise dress and navy cloak.

'What. . . what's happening?' she said, looking round. 'Who are you, my dear?'

Gwen could hear the raven's shrieks getting louder below.

'Hurry up, Gwen!' Flora exclaimed from below them. 'He's almost free!'

'I'm Gwen – Guinevere,' she gasped to Grace. 'Nineve sent me and my cousin Flora to rescue you, and help you get back to Avalon. But I'm afraid we've got to be quick. Morgana is trying to stop us – she's sent that giant raven to attack us.' Gwen pointed quickly to where the raven was still struggling to free itself from the net. 'I've trapped it for now, but it will get free at any moment.'

Grace looked alarmed. 'What can we do?'

But it was too late to do anything. With a final triumphant shriek the raven ripped away the rest of the net.

'Gwen!' yelled Flora. 'Watch out!'

There was the sound of beating wings and the huge raven appeared in the sky. Seeing Grace standing on the ledge with Gwen, it screamed furiously.

Gwen grabbed another arrow and notched it on to her bowstring. She fired it, but the raven managed to dodge out of the way. The arrow flew by harmlessly, falling into the sea below. The raven continued towards them, its talons reaching out. *This is it,* thought Gwen. *It's going to get us!*

Suddenly she heard Grace chanting out a spell:

'Spirits of the sapphire sea
Heed my call, and please help me.'

Gwen glanced round. Grace was looking out at the sea, her hands raised. Almost as the last word left her mouth, an enormous wave began to form. It swelled upwards until it looked like a wall of water. White foam topped it. Gwen gasped. The giant wave grew and swelled as it raced towards

the cliff. Seeing the water coming, the raven cawed in alarm and flew upwards.

'Wait, what about Flora?' Gwen cried, realising that her cousin and the boat would be tossed up like a piece of seaweed by the huge wave.

'Do not worry,' said Grace. She called out:

'Bring my friend to safety here,
'Please be gentle, cause no fear.'

The wave reached the little boat. Gwen's hands
flew to her mouth – but she need not have worried.
The boat was swept up at the top of the wall of
water, but it was held steady. Flora grabbed the
sides as the boat surfed on the top of the wave,
moving towards the ledge where Grace and
Gwen were standing. Suddenly, as Gwen began
to fear that the wave was going to crash over
them, Grace took her hands. 'Trust in Avalon's
magic!' she said calmly.

Gwen felt a moment of shock as the water
enveloped her, but before she could panic, she felt
the hands of invisible spirits holding on to her,

sweeping her gently up towards the very top of the cliffs. Then she was bursting out of the water, launching up for a moment into the air, before tumbling gently down on to the soft grass at the top of the cliff. As she stood up, she saw that Grace and Flora had landed safely beside her.

Gwen gasped and looked over the edge of the cliff as another wave grew from the sea. But unlike the gentle water that had carried them to safety, this wave splashed viscously high into the air – so high that it hit the raven full on! He gave a shriek of surprise and then, with a miserable caw, the giant bird turned and flapped away in defeat, water dripping off his beak, his claws and his wings.

For a moment there was silence as the sea settled, leaving only small waves rippling at its surface. Grace leaped gracefully to her feet. 'Thank you!' she called out to the water. Then she spun around. 'And thank you both for freeing me!' she said to Gwen and Flora, hugging them.

'I'm just glad we managed to,' said Gwen, smiling broadly.

'It was certainly scary,' Flora said, her voice

still a little shaky. 'I thought I was going to be drowned, and that the raven was going to hurt you both!'

Grace took Flora's hands. 'It was so brave of you both. Just rowing out and climbing the

cliff was courageous enough without having Morgana's enchanted raven to deal with.'

'He was horrible,' said Flora with a shudder.

'Where's the boat?' Gwen said suddenly.

'Do not worry,' Grace said. 'It is safe.' She gestured towards the edge of the cliff. Gwen looked over and saw that the tide had retreated again, and the little boat had come safely to rest back on the small patch of shingle at the base of the cliffs.

Gwen breathed a sigh of relief. 'Thank you, Grace. We can fetch it later when the tide goes out a bit more. I wouldn't want to lose it.'

'First, Grace should get back to Avalon before Morgana realises what's happened,' Flora said anxiously. She turned towards the beautiful young woman. 'Your sisters Sophia, Lily, Isabella and Amelia are all there already.'

Grace cried out in delight. 'So they are safe!'

'Yes! And we'll rescue your other three sisters who are still trapped as soon as possible,' promised Gwen.

Grace looked very grateful. 'Thank you from the bottom of my heart. You girls are so very brave. You are right – I should return home right away. How far are we from Avalon?'

'Quite far,' answered Gwen. 'It's a day's ride away for us, but you could use your magic to get back there straight away. You don't have to wait – we will come and see you all very soon.'

Grace nodded. 'I shall go then. If I stay here I will only bring danger to you. Morgana will no doubt try and capture me again given the chance.'

'We'll come and see you when we return to my home. It's not far from the Lake,' said Flora.

'Before I go, I would like to give you a small

token of my gratitude.' Grace pointed at the necklace around Gwen's neck. 'I can see that my sisters have all given you gifts that may well help you one day. I shall add a gem of my own.' Her eyes fell on a nearby small pool of clear water that had been left by the wave breaking on the cliff and she smiled.

Kneeling down beside the pool, Grace passed her hand over the top of the water and whispered a word. The surface of the water started to swirl. It went faster and faster until a spring bubbled up from its centre. As it did so, a blue gem floated up and bobbed gently. It sparkled like the ocean in sunlight. Grace reached down and delicately picked up the gemstone. 'Thank you,' she whispered.

The waterspout vanished, and Grace straightened up and turned to the girls. 'This

sapphire is to add to the other gems, Guinevere.
I hope it may come in useful one day.' She held
it out and the gem floated towards Gwen. There
was a blue flash, and the next moment the sapphire
was attached to her necklace, nestling alongside
the amber gem.

Gwen's fingers went to it. 'Thank you!'

Grace hugged Gwen and then Flora. 'For the moment, my friends, farewell. I shall tell Nineve and my sisters everything that has passed here today.' She raised her hands. 'To Avalon!' she cried, clapping them together. There was a bright silvery-blue flash and then the space where she had been standing was suddenly empty.

Gwen and Flora breathed out huge sighs of relief

'Oh, Gwen,' Flora said, hugging her. 'I'm so glad we managed to free her.'

'Just three more Spell Sisters left now,' said Gwen. 'Morgana's going to be furious.'

Flora nodded. 'We should probably leave here ourselves,' she said.

Gwen picked up her bow and slung it over her shoulder, and they set off across the cliff top back towards the manor house.

Flora gave her cousin a sideways look as they walked. 'So you didn't need your old bow after all?'

'No.' Gwen sighed happily. 'I suppose I didn't!' She stroked her new bow. 'I'll always love my old one, but I think I *will* start to use this one from now on. You were right – I don't need my old bow to bring me luck!'

Flora smiled at her. 'I wonder what Nineve will say when Grace returns.'

'And what Avalon will look like when Grace joins her sisters there,' Gwen agreed. Every time a sister returned the island changed slightly, became less barren and more magical. 'I wish we could see it. . .'

'Gwen! Your pendant! Look!' Flora said, pointing.

Gwen looked down. Her pendant was sparkling with light. Nineve's face appeared in it.

'My friends,' said Nineve, smiling at them through the pendant. 'Grace is here with me. She has just returned.'

The picture changed and Gwen and Flora could see the figures of Nineve and Grace standing together on the surface of the lake. Grace waved. 'I thought after all your adventures you would like to watch as Grace returns to Avalon!' said Nineve.

'Oh, yes please!' the girls breathed.

They stared into the pendant. The purple mist covering the island shifted and then parted,

allowing Nineve and Grace to walk hand-in-hand towards Avalon. Then Grace stepped out of the water on to the rocky shore of the island, leaving Nineve standing on the Lake's surface.

'Look at Avalon now!' Gwen whispered to Flora. When they had first seen the island the land had been dried up, the trees bare-branched and the house up the path from the shore empty and deserted. But now grass was growing over the island again, leaves and blossom were appearing on the apple trees, insects were buzzing and glittering streams were winding across the island, the water rushing merrily over rocks and stones. The house had smoke coming from its chimneys and they could see warm light in its windows. Gwen and Flora watched as Grace ran up the path towards the house.

The door flew open and Isabella, Sophia,

Lily and Amelia, the four sisters whom Gwen and Flora had already freed, came running out. They threw their arms around their sister, exclaiming in delight as happy tears ran down Grace's face. Flora and Gwen looked at one another, their own eyes welling with happiness too.

Nineve's face swum into view in the pendant again. 'Thank you,' she said warmly. 'You have brought Grace and her magic back to Avalon. You have been very brave.'

'But we must get all the sisters back,' said Gwen determinedly.

'I shall contact you again as soon as I discover the whereabouts of the three remaining sisters,' Nineve said to her. 'Until then, stay safe!'

'Goodbye, Nineve!' Gwen and Flora called.

The image of Nineve faded and the pendant returned to normal.

'Oh, wasn't it lovely seeing Grace arrive back home!' said Flora happily.

'It was.' Gwen smiled. 'Come on. We should go home too.'

9
A Special Surprise

'Oh, my goodness, where have you two been?' Gwen's mother exclaimed, looking at Gwen and Flora's wet hair and damp dresses as they walked into the hall. She was sitting with Eleanor playing a board game by the fire. 'You both look like little drowned rats!' she said with a chuckle.

'Yes, you're soaking!' giggled Eleanor. 'Been

having an adventure?'

'We . . . um . . . we went for a walk by the beach,' said Gwen. 'And suddenly a huge wave came out of nowhere.'

'Like it was magic?' Eleanor asked eagerly.

'A bit,' said Gwen, a twinkle in her eye. 'The water went all over us.'

'You poor things,' said Gwen's mother. 'You must go and get changed. Did you have a nice walk apart from the wave getting you?'

Gwen nodded. If only she knew!

'It's not fair!' sighed Eleanor. 'I play by the beach every day and nothing exciting ever happens to me.'

'Well, apart from falling out of apple trees,' her mother said dryly.

'That's not exciting!' protested Eleanor. 'I mean proper exciting things. Gwen gets to live in a huge castle, and go to tournaments, and shoot with a bow and arrow! I don't do anything fun like that.'

Her mother kissed her head. 'Patience, my dear. I know it seems like Gwen has all the fun at the moment, but life will get more exciting for you too as you get older. When you're ten you'll go away to your Aunt Matilda's castle as well.'

Eleanor huffed. 'But that's ages away!'

Gwen gave her a sympathetic look. She could remember feeling just the same when she was her sister's age.

Eleanor turned to her. 'I wish you weren't going back tomorrow. I wish you and Flora could stay for longer.'

'I know,' Gwen replied. 'But I'll make sure I come and visit again. I won't leave it so long next time.'

Eleanor nodded but still looked unhappy.

Gwen suddenly had a perfect idea. 'Wait here!' she said.

She ran upstairs to her chamber and returned with her old bow in her hands. 'Here,' she said, offering it to Eleanor.

Eleanor gasped, and put her hand over her mouth. 'But, Gwen, that's yours. Why are you giving it to me?'

'To keep,' Gwen said with a smile. 'It's too small for me now. You can have it if you want.'

Eleanor stared at her. 'What? Really?

You really mean it?'

Gwen looked quickly at her mother to check it was all right. Her mother nodded and Gwen smiled at her sister. 'Yes, I do. I've got my new bow now, so you can have this one. It means that when Flora and I have to go back and your foot is better you *will* have something fun to do. You'll be able to start learning to shoot properly!'

Eleanor's eyes sparkled like stars. 'Oh, that's amazing! I've always, always wanted to learn to shoot, but all the bows here are too big for me. I want to be as good as you.'

'I bet you soon will be if you practice lots,' Gwen said. 'We'll be able to have competitions when I come home next!'

Eleanor put the bow down and reached up to give Gwen a hug. Gwen squeezed her back tightly. 'This is the best present I've ever had,

Gwen! Thank you!'

In that moment, Gwen knew that there was no one in the world she would rather see using her bow than her feisty, brave sister. 'It's a very special bow,' she whispered. 'Maybe now it's yours, you'll end up in an adventure of your own too!'

The two sisters exchanged grins and parted. Gwen joined Flora.

'Now, you two really should go and get changed out of those damp clothes,' her mother said. 'Go on! Upstairs, both of you!'

They hurried up the staircase to the bedchamber.

'I'm really glad you gave your bow to Eleanor,' said Flora.

Gwen nodded happily. 'Me too.' She had thought she would never part with her old bow,

but now it felt like exactly the right thing to do.

They reached her chamber. Sun was streaming in through the small window. 'Well, another Spell Sister rescued and another adventure over,' said Flora with a contented sigh. 'I can't wait until we get back and go to the Lake again.'

'And find out where the remaining sisters are trapped,' said Gwen. She touched her magic pendant. 'Just call us when you need us, Nineve,' she whispered. 'We'll be waiting.'

The pendant winked and glittered in the rays of the sun.

In a Forest Clearing

Morgana Le Fay stood in the forest inside her enormous hollowed-out oak tree. She was staring into a black crystal ball. Her body tensed. 'No!' she hissed as she watched the scene in the ball unfold. 'No!' With a shriek she threw the ball outside. It crashed into a tree trunk and exploded into pieces, with a loud bang. Swinging around, Morgana's eyes fell on an ornate jug in the corner of her dark lair. She reached down and picked it up, tilting it to pour the water out with one hand. With the other, she stretched her fingers towards the steady stream, trying to conjure it to move and bend at her will. It was no use. She'd lost the power to control water.

Morgana, screamed with fury and stormed out into the clearing around her lair, pacing like a panther in a cage. 'This cannot be. They cannot have freed another sister,' she muttered, her eyes flashing.

There was a shrieking caw and the sound of large wings beating. Her enchanted raven came swooping into the clearing, still huge and black. Morgana's hands shot out and a ball of green fire burst from her fingertips and hit him.

For a moment the bird was lit up with an electric green light, and then he shrank back down to his normal size. 'You failed me!' Morgana shrieked. 'You let those wretched girls free another sister!'

The raven landed on the grass. He cawed anxiously.

'Get out of my sight!' Morgana screamed. She shot another ball of green flames at him. The raven hopped back, dodging it just in time. Flapping his wings, he rose into the sky.

'Go!' hissed Morgana shooting more fire at him. The raven flew hastily away leaving just a few black feathers floating to the ground.

Morgana glared after him and then took a breath. 'It matters not. Three of my sisters are still trapped and the eclipse grows closer. Avalon is still within my grasp and I will make sure that those girls will not thwart my plans again.' Her eyes narrowed. 'I shall make sure of it.'

Turning around, she swept angrily into her oak-tree lair.

Read on for a sneak peek of the next SPELL SISTERS adventure!

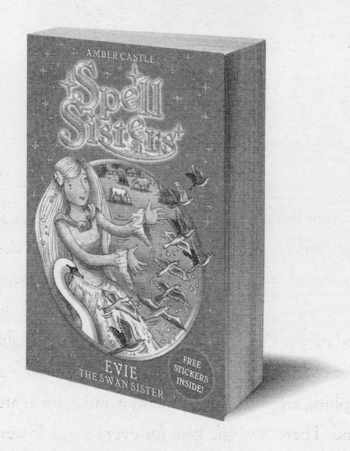

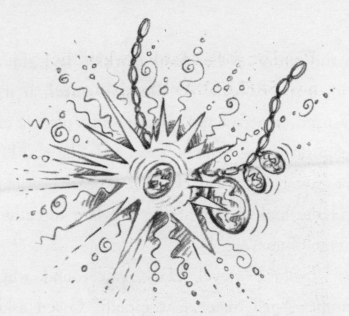

Light flooded into the barn through the small window, the rays of sunlight catching the dust that danced in the air. The girls went over to the window and Gwen pulled the large blue pendant out of her cloak. It was hung on a bright silver chain with five gems clustered beside it – a sapphire, an emerald, an amethyst and a fire agate stone. There was one gem for every sister Gwen and Flora had freed. The large blue pendant in the centre of the chain sparkled and glowed with a silvery light. As the girls stared at it, a mist passed across the surface and a picture of a beautiful young woman appeared. She had long chestnut hair held back with a pearl headband and she looked out of the pendant directly at them. 'Guinevere! Flora!'

'Hello Nineve! Have you found where another Spell Sister is trapped?' Gwen asked eagerly.

'Yes. It is Evie, the Swan Sister. Come to the Lake and I shall show you.'

'We'll come straight away!'

Nineve smiled. 'Thank you.'

Her image disappeared in another swirl of mist.

'Evie the Swan Sister,' Flora breathed. All the sisters had incredible powers, but Morgana had stolen their magic for herself when she captured them. 'I wonder where she's trapped?'

Gwen looked excited. 'Let's go to the Lake and find out!'

The two girls hurried away from the castle and down the hill towards the forest. Luckily no one stopped them or asked where they were going. As they ran into the trees, shadows closed around them. The thick canopy of leaves overhead shut out the sunlight, and Gwen had to grab Flora's hand as she stumbled over a tree root.

'Careful!' Gwen gasped.

'I'm fine, I'm just always so clumsy!' exclaimed Flora. She hurried on a few paces but then slipped again on a patch of damp leaves. She grabbed a tree trunk to save herself.

'Should we call Moonlight?' Gwen suggested with a smile. 'He'll get us to the Lake in no time.' Flora nodded, looking relieved.

Gwen whistled and moments later, a horse's answering whinny rang out. They heard the sound of cantering hooves and then a snow-white stallion burst through the trees. His mane and tail hung in beautiful silky silver strands.

He trotted over and pushed his head against Gwen's chest.

'Moonlight!' Gwen sighed happily and buried her head in his soft mane. She loved all horses but Moonlight was special. On their very first adventure, she had fed him a special apple from Avalon and it had given him magical powers. He could gallop faster than any normal horse, and he seemed to understand almost everything they said. Moonlight lifted his nose to her face and blew out softly.

'We need to get to the Lake,' Gwen told him. 'Will you take us there please?'

Moonlight whickered softly, and Gwen took hold of his mane and vaulted on to his back. Then she steered him over to a fallen log. Flora stood on it and managed to scramble up behind Gwen.

'Hold on tight,' Gwen said. Flora wrapped her arms around Gwen's waist, and off they went!

Moonlight surged forward, his mane swirling around them as he galloped through the trees. He swerved and dodged as the girls hung on, trusting that he would take them to the Lake safely.

Within minutes, Moonlight came to a stop. The silvery lake stretched out in front of them, with a purple mist swirling over it, hiding the island of Avalon.

As they watched, Nineve, the Lady of the Lake, rose up through the waters until she seemed to be standing on its surface. Her long hair reached all the way down to her feet and her blue and green gown glimmered. She greeted them warmly. 'Gwen! Flora! Thank you for coming so quickly.'

Gwen and Flora dismounted. Nineve could

not leave the water – she had cast a spell on the Lake preventing Morgana from crossing it, but it would only work while she was in the water.

'What have you found out, Nineve?' Gwen asked, going to the edge of the water.

'You said the next sister is called Evie?' Flora said, following her.

'Yes, that is right. Evie the Swan Sister, whose magic controls all the birds in the kingdom, I believe she is trapped somewhere nearby. Look!' Nineve clasped her hands and held them up high in the air. She whispered a word and then, bringing her hands down slowly, she opened them to reveal a white swan feather lying across her palms. It glimmered like a fresh pearl.

Gwen felt goose bumps prickle across her skin. She loved watching Nineve do magic.

Taking the feather, Nineve stroked it gently

across the surface of the water by her feet. The water started to swirl round and round like a mini whirlpool. Nineve touched the centre with the swan feather and suddenly the water was completely still. Gwen saw a picture appear in the surface.

'What is it?' said Flora, peering closer.

'It's a stable door,' said Gwen. It was painted red and was at the end of a row of stables.

Nineve nodded. 'I believe it must be near to where Evie is imprisoned – that's why the magic is showing it to us.'

'We've got to find it!' declared Gwen.

'But how?' Flora asked. 'It could be anywhere. There are so many stables in the kingdom.'

'I feel as if it is somewhere nearby,' said Nineve. 'But I do not know its exact location.'

Gwen's heart sank. It would take for ever

to check all the nearby stables. She looked at the picture, searching for any kind of clue. Her eyes fell on three horseshoes nailed to the wall of the stable block. They were arranged in a pattern, one on top, two below. Gwen felt something tug at her memory. Stablemen often believed that horseshoes would bring good luck and keep evil spirits away, but there was something about the particular arrangement of these ones...

'It's a stud!' she realised. 'A place where horses are bred and sold. Three horseshoes in that pattern show it's a place where horses are bred. There are only about three studs within a day's ride. Maybe Evie is at one of them?'

'It's worth a try. We could go and visit each of them to check,' said Flora, but then she frowned. 'But how will we do that? Young ladies don't buy horses. We can't just visit stud yards without it seeming strange.'

Flora was right, they needed some kind of a plan. 'Maybe you can persuade your father you need a new pony?' Gwen suggested, 'Or... That's it! Arthur!' she gasped. '

'Arthur?' Flora echoed. 'What's he got to do with this?'

'Remember he told us that he was going to look at horses today with Jacob? We could ask if we could go with them. Jacob won't mind, and I'm sure Arthur will say yes if I ask him.'

Flora grabbed her hands. 'Oh, that's a perfect idea!'

'It does sound like a very good plan,' Nineve said warmly, but then her face grew serious. 'Still, remember to watch out for Morgana. With only three Spell Sisters left in her power, she will be more determined than ever to stop you. She is

bound to be protecting every sister with her powers. Be very careful in case she attacks.'

'We will be,' Gwen promised. She knew it was no idle warning. Morgana had tried to stop their rescue attempts several times, with very dangerous results.

'Goodbye, Nineve,' said Flora. 'Hopefully we'll be back soon with Evie.'

'I hope so too.' Nineve lifted her hand in a farewell. 'May Avalon keep you safe.'

The girls watched as she sank down slowly into the water. It rippled and then she was gone, with just a single swan feather left floating on the surface.

Will Gwen and Flora be able to rescue Evie?

Read the rest of

EVIE

THE SWAN SISTER

to find out!

MAKE YOUR OWN
SPECIAL SAILBOAT!

Follow these simple instructions to make a cute sailing boat that
really floats. It's great fun to make a few boats and race them
with your friends. Hopefully you won't face waters that are as
stormy as those battled by Gwen and Flora in the story!

What you'll need:

+ A wide plastic lid (the best ones are the lids of margarine/
  butter tubs) or an empty plastic vegetable tray
+ A drinking straw
+ Paper
+ Superglue
+ Scissors

*Remember to
always be careful when
you're working with scissors and
glue or ask a grown-up
to help you.*

HOW TO MAKE YOUR BOAT:

1. Glue the drinking straw to the middle of plastic lid/tray so that it stands up vertically – this will form the mast for your sail.

2. Cut your paper into a square and make two small holes, one at the top and one at the bottom of the piece of paper. This is going to form your sail, so try to make the holes as central as possible to ensure that it isn't uneven.

3. Slide the paper over your straw, threading it through the two holes.

4. Open the piece of paper so the sail forms a 'c' shape.

5. Now you have a finished boat! Put it to the test by sailing it in your bath or sink. Blow on the sail to make it go!

TOP TIPS

✛ Try using a piece of fabric instead of paper for the sail to create a really pretty effect, or decorate your plastic tray with stickers or felt-tip pens - but remember to only decorate the areas that won't get wet!

✛ If you don't have any strong glue you can use a blob of Blu-Tack to secure your straw.

VISIT WWW.SPELLSISTERS.CO.UK AND

Plus lots of other enchanted extras!

Spell Sisters news

Explore Avalon

More about Gwen and Flora's quest

Spell Sister profiles

Activity sheets

Wallpapers

Your chance to get in touch with us

ENTER THE MAGICAL WORLD OF AVALON!

Spell Sisters